THE UNOFFICIAL

MINECRAFT™ TOOL KIT

SNOW STOPPING YOU

WITH MINECRAFT™

JOEY DAVEY   JONATHAN GREEN   JULIET STANLEY

Gareth Stevens
PUBLISHING

Please visit our website, **www.garethstevens.com**.
For a free color catalog of all our high-quality books,
call toll free 1-800-542-2595 or fax 1-877-542-2596.

Cataloging-in-Publication Data
Names: Davey, Joey. | Green, Jonathan. | Stanley, Juliet.
Title: Snow stopping you with Minecraft™ / Joey Davey,
Jonathan Green, and Juliet Stanley.
Description: New York : Gareth Stevens Publishing, 2018. |
Series: The unofficial Minecraft™ tool kit | Includes index.
Identifiers: LCCN ISBN 9781538217160 (pbk.) |
ISBN 9781538217115 (library bound) | ISBN 9781538217061 (6 pack)
Subjects: LCSH: Minecraft (Game)--Juvenile literature. | Minecraft (Video game)--
Handbooks, manuals, etc.--Juvenile literature. |
Classification: LCC GV1469.M55 D38 2018 | DDC 794.8--dc23

Published in 2018 by
Gareth Stevens Publishing
111 East 14th Street, Suite 349
New York, NY 10003

Designed and packaged by: Dynamo Limited
Built and written by: Joey Davey, Jonathan Green, and Juliet Stanley

Printed in the United States of America
CPSIA compliance information: Batch CW18GS: For further information contact
Gareth Stevens, New York, New York at 1-800-542-2595.

CONTENTS

WELCOME
TO THE WONDERFUL WORLD OF
MINECRAFT!

If you're reading this, then you're probably already familiar with the fantastic game of building blocks and going on adventures. If you're not, go download Minecraft now and try it out!

Courtesy of IAmNewAsWell

READY?

OKAY, LET'S GET STARTED!

« THE AIM OF THE GAME »

This book has projects of three different difficulty ratings, which will help you hone your building skills. Each project has clear step-by-step instructions. You'll also find expert tips, like this one . . .

One of the greatest things about Minecraft – apart from being able to explore randomly generated worlds – is that you can build amazing things, from the simplest home to the grandest castle. This book will help you become a master builder, capable of building your own epic Minecraft masterpieces.

EXPERT TIP!

CREATIVE MODE vs SURVIVAL MODE

If you build in Creative mode, you'll have all the blocks you need to complete your build, no matter how outlandish. However, if you like more of a challenge, why not build in Survival mode? Just remember – you'll have to mine all your resources first, and you will also be kept busy crafting weapons and armor to fend off dangerous mobs of zombies and creepers!

Courtesy of crpeh

FAIL TO PREPARE AND PREPARE TO FAIL

If you're building in Survival mode, before you get going, you'll need to set up your hotbar so that items such as torches, tools, and weapons are all within easy reach. You'll also want to make sure that you're building on a flat surface.

For the best results, use Minecraft PC to complete all of the step-by-step builds in this book.

Before you start, you'll need to mine all your resources, and before you can do that, you'll need to sort out your Tool Kit . . . turn the page for further help.

Courtesy of swifsampson

EXPERT TIP!

ALL THAT GLITTERS

If you're planning on creating a Minecraft masterpiece, you'll want some super-special materials. To find rare ores, like diamonds, mine a staircase to Level 14 and then strip-mine the area. But remember – you'll need an iron or diamond pickaxe to mine most ores. If you use any other type of tool, you'll destroy the block without getting anything from it.

Courtesy of Cornbass

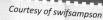

STAYING SAFE ONLINE

Minecraft is one of the most popular games in the world, and you should have fun while you're playing it. However, it is just as important to stay safe when you're online.

Top tips for staying safe are:
≫ turn off chat
≫ find a kid-friendly server
≫ watch out for viruses and malware
≫ set a game-play time limit
≫ tell a trusted adult what you're doing

TOOLED UP!

Before you get cracking – or should that be crafting? – you're going to need to make sure that you're set with all the tools you'll need.

« CUSTOMIZE YOUR HOTBAR »

Your inventory is the place where everything you mine and collect is stored. You can access it at any time during the game.

When you exit your inventory, a hotbar will appear at the bottom of the screen, made up of a line of nine hotkey slots. Think of this as your mini-inventory where you can keep the things you use most frequently.

It's vitally important to take time to organize your hotbar carefully – in a game of Survival, it might just save your life!

Move an item from your inventory into one of the hotkey slots to assign it. Then, when you select a slot, the item you have placed in there will automatically appear in your hand, ready for you to use.

« HOT OR NOT »

Always keep at least one weapon and one food source in your hotbar. Also make sure you've got some tools in there. It's always handy to have a pickaxe or two, or perhaps a shovel, depending on what you're planning on mining. A torch will also be handy. Last of all, you want to make sure that you have some basic building materials ready.

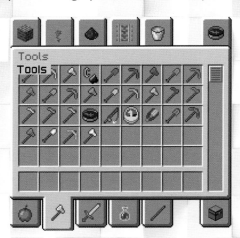

EXPERT TIP!

GO FISH!

Fishing rods are surprisingly useful. You can use them to catch fish, and you can also cast them to set off pressure plates while you stay out of harm's way.

≪ BUILDING BLOCKS ≫

WOOD

Always useful, as you need it to craft many everyday items. In Survival mode, always carry some logs with you — especially if you're going caving, as wood is hard to find underground.

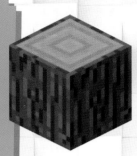

EXPERT TIP!

REDSTONE RAMPAGE

If you want your Minecraft masterpiece to have moving mechanisms, like a roller coaster, you're going to need some redstone. This block allows you to create moving parts, and even circuits.

STONE

The most common block in the game, it is good at keeping creepers at bay. If you're planning on building a castle, stone is what you're going to need — and lots of it!

OBSIDIAN

Other than bedrock, this is the hardest material — and it's completely creeper-proof! You'll need an entire lava source block and 15 seconds with a diamond pick to mine it in Survival mode, though.

BRICK

Harder than stone and can be crafted out of clay, although it does take a long time to craft and will drain your fuel supply.

≪ MIND-BOGGLING BIOMES ≫

The different types of terrain you encounter in Minecraft are called biomes. They range from ice plains and swamps, to deserts and jungles, to oceans and fantasy islands.

Courtesy of Epic Minecraft Seeds

Courtesy of MADbakamono

These biomes will take you to the sky and back, quite literally!

7

UN-BOX YOUR BUILD

The amazing world of Minecraft is made from lots and lots of . . . blocks! But these simple, straight-edged blocks certainly don't stop its biggest fans from building masterpieces that curve, spiral, and defy the cuboid. With a little help and a lot of imagination, you can make even your wildest dream builds come true. Let's take a look at some of the creative possibilities Minecraft has to offer.

« ECCENTRIC ENTRANCES »

Make your entrances unforgettable with lots of different materials, shapes, and a few surprises! The first door is the perfect entrance for a treetop lodge. From a distance it looks like it has been carved out of a tree trunk by woodland creatures. There's a hidden entrance in the second doorway, and the colors created by wool and emerald blocks are totally wild!

« WOW FACTOR WINDOWS »

Why not try your hand at making these stunning windows? Short rows, L-shapes, and single blocks create a circular web within the frame of the first window. Diagonally placed blocks in the second window create curved lines that look like a propeller. But you don't have to stick to square windows – anything is possible in Minecraft!

EXPERT TIP!

SKETCH IT

Being prepared will make building in Minecraft easier and much more fun. You'll have a good idea of what you want your final build to look like, and you'll have given yourself time to think about how to do it. Forget math for a second – grid paper is perfect for planning what to do with all of these blocks!

The dark blue flooring and back wall cleverly disguise this open entrance.

≪ REMARKABLE ≫ ROOFS

Here are three in-spire-ational roofs for you to try! For a look inspired by ancient Chinese architecture, add blocks in the corners of simple roof structures. Or go for a space age design with lava, emerald, diamond, and beacon blocks! Staying hidden is always a good strategy in Survival mode – this last grass roof is the perfect way to disguise your builds.

≪ SENSATIONAL ≫ STRUCTURES

Yes, it's a woolly hat house made from wool blocks! Try recreating this circular structure with lots of different-sized rows. The only rule is: stay symmetrical. This arched bridge is a super-simple structure, and it can be used to add interest to the front of a building, or to un-box square windows. The last building uses columns to support a balcony and to add texture to its surface. This would be a great look for a castle.

EXPERT TIP!

BE INSPIRED

Search online or flip through books to find inspiration for your creations! As well as a myriad of Minecraft buildings, you'll find plenty of weird and wonderful real-life buildings that you can use to help you come up with your very own masterpiece. Happy building, Minecrafters!

THE RULES OF COOL

What's cooler than being cool? Being ice cold, of course! But survival in snow-filled biomes is difficult due to the lack of building materials, like wood, and animals (AKA passive mobs). And there are plenty of hostile mobs, like polar bears, strays, and zombies! As if that wasn't enough, you'll also have to contend with snowstorms and fog!

Still want to visit? Well, there are plenty of snow-dusted environments to choose from in Minecraft . . .

Ice Plains – a large, flat biome with a huge amount of snow. Any source of water open to the sky will be frozen, and trees are few and far between. Fewer passive mobs spawn here than in other biomes, but igloos generate naturally.

Frozen River – you may find this type of river in an Ice Plains biome – it's the only place they generate. The surface is frozen, as you might have already guessed!

Cold Beach – where an Ice Plains biome meets an ocean, you will often find this kind of snowy seaside scene.

Ice Plains Spikes – you're less likely to find this rare variation of the Ice Plains biome. It's populated with large spikes of packed ice, which won't melt in the way normal ice does.

Cold Taiga – this is a snowy variation of the Taiga biome, so it is full of ferns and spruce trees. Watch out for wolves – they spawn naturally here!

EXPERT TIP!

POLAR BEARS

Found in Ice Plains and Ice Spikes biomes, polar bears are usually neutral mobs. However, they will become hostile if they or their cubs are attacked. When threatened, they rear up on their hind legs and strike their attacker using their front paws. It's not so easy to give a polar bear the cold shoulder either, since their swimming speed is faster than the player's, making it difficult to escape from these ice-loving bears.

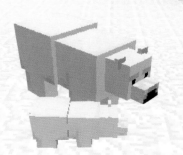

Courtesy of Planet Minecraft

1

2

3

4

≪ N-ICE PLACE! ≫

Part of the appeal of building in a snowy biome is the ability to build igloos. In Survival mode, you'll need to collect the snow using a shovel. Each shovelful will create a snowball, and putting four snowballs together will make one snow block. Once you have enough of these, you can craft your igloo.

EXPERT TIP!

SNOW SOLDIERS

Snow golems are handy utility mobs – build them as your first line of defense while you get working on your snowy structures. It won't take much to build up your own icy army. Stack two snow blocks and pop a pumpkin on the top (a golem will only spawn if the pumpkin is placed last).

EXPERT TIP!

LET IT SNOW

You can create some truly stunning builds in snowy biomes. After all, everything looks better after a dusting of snow.

SNOW STOPPING YOU

IGLOO »

DIFFICULTY
EASY

TIME
1 HOUR

An icy reception awaits you in the snowy biomes of Minecraft, but don't let that stop you from visiting. Basic igloos appear across the landscape or you could follow these steps to build a bigger and better igloo of your very own in s-no-w time at all! Then you'll be free to explore without having to worry how you'll survive the wintry weather . . . or those pesky hostile mobs!

MATERIALS

STEP 1

Cut a round shape in the snow, like the one pictured. Now build a ring of snow blocks around the edges. This forms the base for your igloo.

STEP 2

To create your entrance, first remove one block from the middle of one of your longest walls. Then make your wall two blocks high and add four more blocks on either side of the entrance to extend it, as shown.

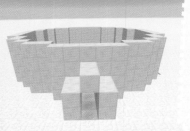

STEP 3

Build your wall one block higher and add two blocks above the entrance to make it snow-proof and snug. Add a smaller ring of blocks on the top as shown.

STEP 4

Build another ring of blocks inside the last one. Then craft another smaller ring above the last, using four rows of five blocks and four single blocks in each corner, as shown. Now it's time to create your roof . . .

STEP 5

Again, build another ring of blocks inside the last one. Then top your roof off with a 5x5 square (with one block missing from each corner). Your igloo is almost complete!

STEP 6

Let's go inside! This igloo is in fact a library with oak-wood-stair chairs and oak wood planks as tables. Place torches, a warming fire, and columns of bookshelf blocks along the walls to make your own snowy study.

EXPERT TIP!

SNOW BLOCK FIREPLACE

In the amazing world of Minecraft, snow blocks don't melt, and that's why you can have a roaring fire right in the middle of your igloo. Be warned, natural snow and ice melt, so make sure your fire has snow blocks you have made or selected from your inventory underneath and around it.

STEP 7

Finally, make your frozen home as safe and secure as possible from bad weather and hostile mobs with some well-placed torches and a sturdy front door. Now you can snuggle up with a good Minecraft book and relax!

POLAR OUTPOST

DIFFICULTY
INTERMEDIATE

TIME
2 HOURS

Snowy landscapes hide many secrets! Animals build their homes beneath the ice and everything is constantly being covered in a fresh dusting of snow. This stunning ice research station provides the perfect base for you to explore and succeed in Minecraft's most extreme biome.

MATERIALS

STEP 1

Build a two-block-high circle in the snow from red clay, with cobblestone-wall supports two blocks high underneath. Place these on ice blocks. This will be your central pod.

STEP 2

Create the floor from white hardened clay. Build up the walls with three layers of red clay, one of glass block and one more of red clay. Then build the roof from four layers of glass block, stepped into a dome as shown.

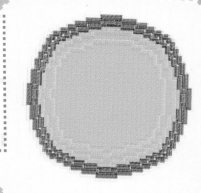

STEP 3

Add a walkway of quartz block to one of the long sides. Then create another smaller circle of red hardened clay, as shown. Don't forget to put this all on cobblestone wall supports with ice-block bottoms, just like you did with the central pod.

STEP 4

Fill in the circle with red hardened clay to create a floor and then add a ring of blocks on the edge to link the structure to the walkway. This is the basis for your first outer pod.

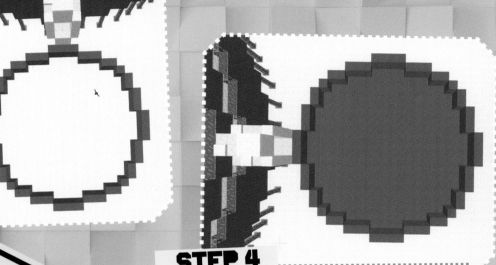

EXPERT TIP!

SNOW PROTECTION

Page 11 tells you how to build snow golems, but do you know how useful they are? They bombard all mobs with a flurry of snowballs, and also distract them so you can attack hostile mobs before they notice you. Snow golems can't damage mobs, but their snowballs can slow them down! But beware – sun, rain and heat will melt your frozen friends.

STEP 5

Build your walls from two more layers of red hardened clay, one layer of glass block, and another layer of red hardened clay. Then build a three-layer domed glass roof, as shown.

STEP 6

Repeat Steps 3, 4, and 5 to create two more pods coming off the sides of your central structure. Your three pods can be customized to provide the perfect place for keeping pets or storing treasures found in the snow.

STEP 7

Build your entrance on the remaining side by adding a short quartz block walkway supported by columns of cobblestone wall on ice blocks. These columns need to be four blocks high. Add two spruce doors and a staircase of stone brick and quartz, as shown.

STEP 8

In one of your pods, add a pool. You can use this to farm squid so you can harvest ink in Survival mode. Simply replace floor blocks with water blocks, making your pool as big as you like.

STEP 9

Turn another pod into a room for brewing potions to give you special powers in Survival mode. Build stone-brick benches around the edges, placing brewing stands and cauldrons at intervals, and a library from bookshelf and stone brick stair.

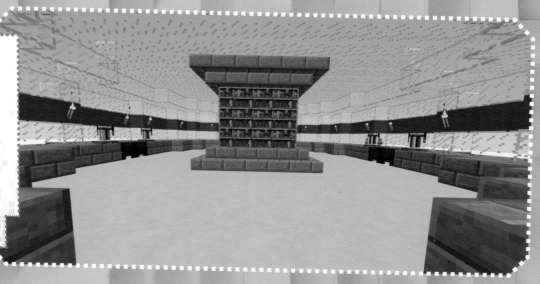

STEP 10

Snow biomes provide very little nourishment, so feed yourself from your final pod! Cover the floor in grass and add rows of dirt for your crops – here you can see melons, pumpkins, and sugarcane. Add bone meal to make things grow.

STEP 11

Build your signaling tower base from 4x4 cyan-hardened-clay blocks. Place an iron block column with two cobblestone-wall antennae on top of this. Finish your signaling tower off with two redstone torches so you can be seen for miles around.

EXPERT TIP!

LIGHT FANTASTIC

Turn your signaling tower into a power generator, giving you five special powers in Survival mode within a certain range – speed, haste, resistance, jump boost, and strength! Remove your antennae, build a diamond pyramid, put some beacons on top and become a Minecraft superhero!

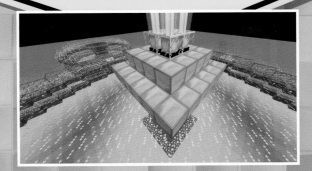

STEP 12

Give an awesome glow effect to your polar outpost by adding torches at regular intervals all around the inside of the walls in each pod. For the finishing touch, build a glowstone rim around the base of your signaling tower.

ICE HOTEL

DIFFICULTY	BUILD TIME
MASTER	**3 HOURS +**

Don't forget your coat for this build! Create a fabulously frosty edifice to celebrate overcoming hostile mobs, chilly temperatures, and a distinct lack of . . . well, everything apart from snow. Once you're done, you'll need to stock your hotel with lots of food and friends. Then, let the fun begin!

STEP 1

Build a 90x90 ice-block square floor with walls 13 blocks high around the edges and curved corners, as pictured. This will make your building look less boxy.

MATERIALS

STEP 2

Remove wall blocks to create the shape for your entrance, as shown. Build an inner wall four blocks back from this following the same shape, and link the walls with more blocks. Add side columns and remove 18 blocks to make your doorway.

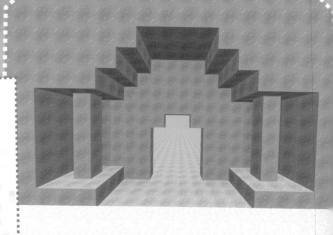

STEP 3

One block down from the top of the wall, build an inside ledge which extends five blocks inwards. This will be a walkway around your castle. Build the foundations for your two rear towers, as shown, then make them 15 blocks high.

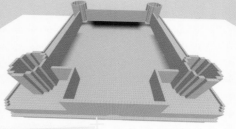

STEP 4

Extend your ledge at the front of the building and position two towers, as shown. Build walls ten blocks high along the inside edge of your walkway, changing direction over the doorway, as pictured. Seven blocks up from the ground, add a single block ledge on the outer wall.

STEP 5

Build the walls until they are 45 blocks high, leaving gaps behind the towers, as shown.

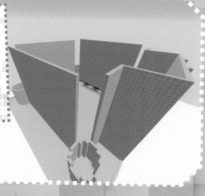

STEP 6

Fill the gaps behind the towers and give them roofs. These should have eight layers of concentric circles, and taper off, as shown.

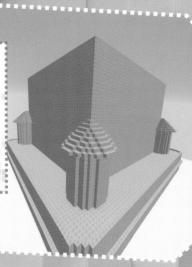

EXPERT TIP!

LET IT SNOW!

Snow will settle on your Minecraft builds and can look really cool against certain materials. Build some sculptures in the snow in front of your ice hotel from a variety of different blocks – wool, stained glass, and clay are some of the most colorful – and check out how the snow grows on them.

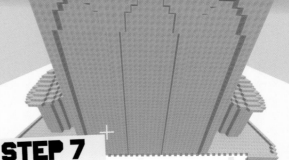

STEP 7

For the front wall decoration, follow this pattern to create three super-cool arches to tower above your entrance.

STEP 8

Protect guests from the elements by adding a canopy over the front door. It should be seven blocks up from the ground (level with the ledge) and have pillars at the front to support it.

STEP 9

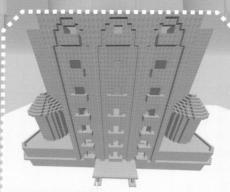

Create a central column of 2x3 block windows with balconies six blocks wide and a three-block gap between each. The side columns should have 3x3 block windows with balconies five blocks wide, as shown.

STEP 10

Lay a flat roof on top of your ice hotel, making sure you create a two-block overhang all the way around the building.

STEP 11

Find the center of your roof by counting in from the outside edges and build the base for your rooftop dome around it.

STEP 12

You don't have to follow the pattern shown and described here, but make sure your walls are circular and symmetrical. Build the walls of your dome 13 blocks high.

EXPERT TIP!

GONE FISHING

You can fish in snow biomes, but if you aren't having any luck, polar bears will drop up to two raw fish if you defeat them. Raw fish can be used to tame ocelots and breed cats, but if you want to increase your energy, you'll need to cook fish before you eat it for the best results.

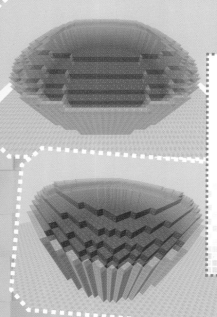

STEP 13

Use glass blocks to build a five-tier roof. Each tier should step up from the last, as shown. The lowest two tiers should be one block wide, the third two blocks and the fourth three blocks wide.

STEP 14

Create a soft glow to welcome visitors on cold winter nights by placing glowstone blocks strategically inside your hotel windows. The more you use, the brighter the glow will be.

STEP 15

Create a stunning checkerboard floor at ground level. Replace ice blocks with glowstone topped with a green stained glass block at regular intervals, as shown. The floor is massive, so this will take time, but the effect will be amazing – your floor will glow!

STEP 16

Build bedroom pods behind your windows. This one is six blocks high, ten wide, and eight long. Add glowstone in each corner for lighting and leave a four-block entrance at the back of the pod for easy access.

STEP 17

Build a ladder from each pod down to ground level. Make these from ice blocks with ladder placed against them, as shown. The basics of this massive build are complete – now you can customize to your heart's content!

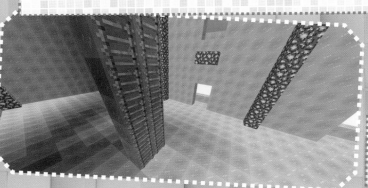

Your ice hotel is now ready for visitors!

GLOSSARY

The world of Minecraft is one that comes with its own set of special words. Here are just some of them.

《 BIOME 》

A region in a Minecraft world with special geographical features, plants, and weather conditions. There are forest, jungle, desert, and snow biomes, and each one contains different resources and numbers of mobs.

《 COLUMN 》

A series of blocks placed on top of each other.

《 DIAGONAL 》

A line of blocks joined corner to corner that looks like a staircase.

《 HOTBAR 》

The selection bar at the bottom of the screen, where you put your most useful items for easy access during Survival mode.

《 INVENTORY 》

This is a pop-up menu containing tools, blocks and other Minecraft items.

《 MOB 》

Short for "mobile," a mob is a moving Minecraft creature with special behaviors. Villagers, animals, and monsters are all mobs, and they can be friendly, like sheep and pigs, or hostile, like creepers. All spawn or breed and some – like wolves and horses – are tamable.

《 ROW 》

A horizontal line of blocks.

FURTHER INFORMATION

BOOKS

Minecraft: Guide to Creative by Mojang AB and The Official Minecraft Team. Del Rey, 2017.

Minecraft: Guide to Exploration by Mojang AB and The Official Minecraft Team. Del Ray, 2017.

Minecraft: The Complete Handbook Collection by Stephanie Mitton and Paul Soares Jr. Scholastic, 2015.

WEBSITES

Visit the official Minecraft website to get started!
https://minecraft.net/en-us/

Explore over 600 kid-friendly Minecraft videos at this awesome site!
https://www.cleanminecraftvideos.com

INDEX

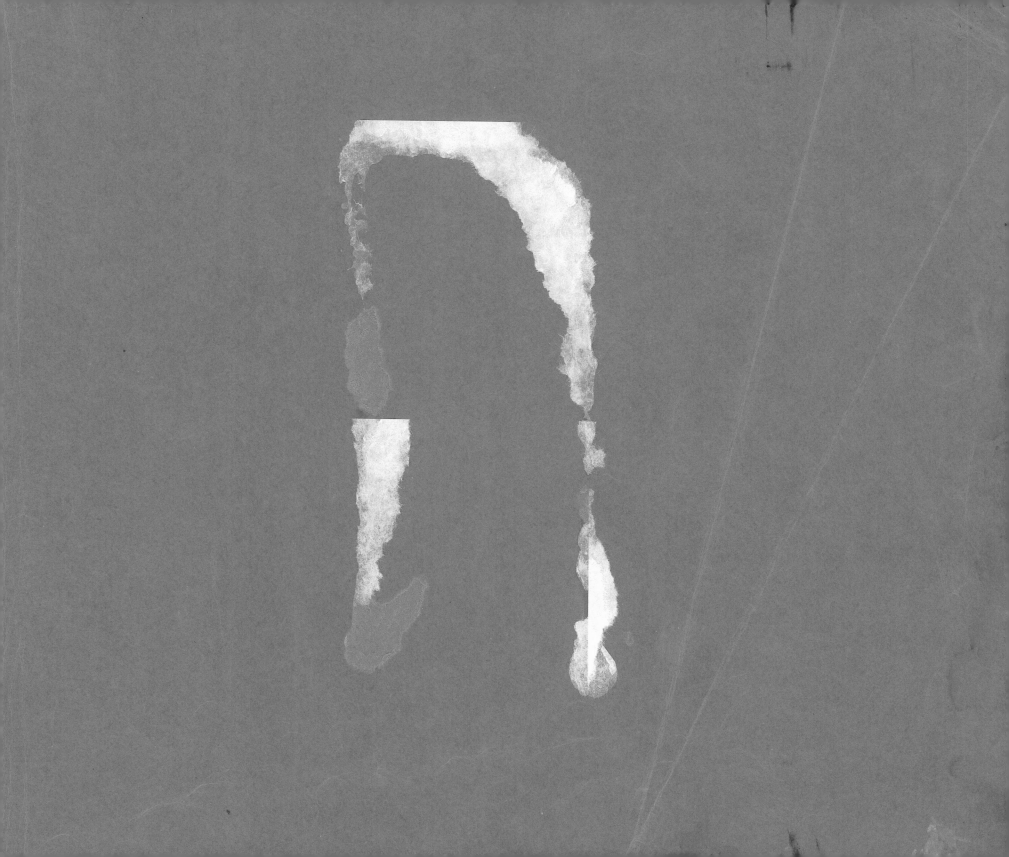